READ ALONE *Get set with Read Alone!*

This entertaining series is designed for all new readers who want to start reading a whole book on their own.

The stories are lively and fun, with lots of illustrations and clear, large type, to make first solo reading a perfect pleasure!

Leon Rosselson

Rosa's Grandfather Sings Again

Illustrated by Norman Young

VIKING

JF

VIKING

Published by the Penguin Group
Penguin Books Ltd, 27 Wrights Lane, London W8 5TZ, England
Viking Penguin, a division of Penguin Books USA Inc.
375 Hudson Street, New York, New York 10014, USA
Penguin Books Australia Ltd, Ringwood, Victoria, Australia
Penguin Books Canada Ltd, 2801 John Street, Markham, Ontario, Canada L3R 1B4
Penguin Books (NZ) Ltd, 182–190 Wairau Road, Auckland 10, New Zealand

Penguin Books Ltd, Registered Offices: Harmondsworth, Middlesex, England

First published 1991
10 9 8 7 6 5 4 3 2 1

Filmset in Times (Linotron 202) by Rowland Phototypesetting Ltd,
Bury St Edmunds, Suffolk
Printed in Great Britain by
Butler & Tanner Ltd, Frome and London

A CIP catalogue record for this book is available from the British Library

ISBN 0–670–83599–4

Contents

What a Performance!

"Once upon a time," said Grandfather.

"When was that, Grandad?"

"When I was a boy," said Grandfather.

"When was that?" asked Rosa.

"Yesterday," said Grandfather. "And if you don't stop asking questions, this story will take until tomorrow."

Rosa pressed her lips together tight.

"Now where was I?" Grandfather looked puzzled.

"Once upon a time," Rosa whispered.

"That's right," said Grandfather. "I was boiling my smalls."

Rosa's eyes opened wide.

"My smalls," said Grandfather. "That's the way I like to do my washing. That's the way we always did it. Washing-machines be blowed! We didn't need washing-

machines. Boil the dirt out of
them. That's the way to do it."

"That's the way to do it,"
repeated Rosa after him.

"And while they were
boiling away on the stove, I sat
down for a little rest in my old

rocking-chair. And do you
know what?"

"What, Grandad?"

"Must have fallen asleep,"
said Grandfather. "Must have
let all the water boil out," said
Grandfather. "But I knew
what to do. I held my breath,

charged into the kitchen and turned off the gas. Then I threw my poor old burnt-out tub and all the smoky clothes into the kitchen sink."

"That was brave," said Rosa.

"It was," said Grandfather. "Then I opened the front door to let the steam out. And what do you think I found there?"

"What, Grandad?"

"The fire brigades," said Grandfather. "Somebody had called the fire brigades. Nincompoops! And all my neighbours were lining the stairs and leaning over the

banisters. Mrs Samuels was there, of course. 'We thought you were on fire,' she said. 'Do I look as if I'm on fire?' I said.

"Then the Chief Fireman went into the kitchen and had a look at my tub. 'This old thing's a goner,' he said. 'I could have told you that,' I said. 'You sure you're all right, Grandad?' said the fireman. 'Of course I'm all right,' I said. Then Mrs Samuels piped up again. 'Maybe we should call a doctor,' she said. 'I don't need a doctor,' I said. 'Listen. I'll show you I'm all right.' "

"And did you?" asked Rosa.

"I did," said Grandad. "I showed them. I sang them a song right there. In the hallway. What a performance! What applause! 'Never heard anything like it,' the fireman laddie said."

"What did you sing?" asked Rosa.

Grandfather stood up, climbed on a chair, spread his arms and sang at the top of his voice: "You are my heart's delight, I think of you the whole night through . . ."

Just then Rosa's mother walked into the room. "What's all this noise?" she said. "I can't hear myself think."

"Grandad's singing a song," said Rosa.

"I can hear that," said Rosa's mother. "But why's he doing it, that's what I want to know?"

Grandfather and Rosa said nothing.

"Time for bed, Rosa," said
Rosa's mother. "Kiss your
grandad good night." Going
up the stairs to bed, Rosa's
mother asked, "What's he been
telling you, your old
grandad?"

"Just a story," said Rosa.

"You shouldn't believe everything Grandad tells you," said Rosa's mother.

But that night, in the deep silence of the night, Rosa dreamed that she was standing with Grandad on the roof of his block of flats, and they were singing together the most beautiful song. And down below, a thousand children, dressed in the uniform of the fire brigades, were staring up at them, open-mouthed and applauding wildly. What a performance!

Grandfather, a Tiger and a Parrot

Rosa and her grandfather were walking back to Grandfather's flat one Thursday after school. "Grandad, my mum said we could go to the zoo on Sunday. If it's a nice day. Do you want to come?"

"Well, I don't know," said Grandfather. "I don't hold

with zoos. Too many cages. She's only a bird in a gilded cage, a beautiful sight to see," he sang, and all the shoppers hurrying along the street turned to look at him suspiciously and then turned away as he sang on, "You may think she's happy and free from care, she's not though she seems to be –"

"But I like seeing the monkeys," said Rosa, puzzled. "And the bears. And the elephants. When I was small, I used to call them 'effelants'. Don't you want to see the elephants?"

"Oh, I've seen the elephants," said Grandad. "In the jungle. That's the place to see elephants."

Rosa's brown eyes opened wide. "Have you, Grandad? Have you really? Tell me about it, Grandad. Tell me." And she pulled at his arm excitedly.

"Hold your horses, my little one," he said. "I'm a bit too puffed for storytelling now. I'm not as young as I was, you know. Wait till we're home. Then I'll tell you a story about elephants – and tigers – that'll make your hair curl."

And so when they were
sitting down at the table in
Grandfather's kitchen, eating
their tea of brown bread and
butter and cheese and
cucumber and tomatoes and
jam and cakes, Rosa asked her
grandfather again to tell her
about the elephants and the
tigers in the jungle.

Grandfather finished
chewing his bread and cheese
before he answered: "It was in
the war. And this cheese
doesn't taste like it used to. We
used to have proper cheese in
my day, cut in the shop before
your eyes, instead of this

soapy-looking stuff all wrapped up in plastic."

"But what about the elephants and the tigers?" Rosa said impatiently.

"In the war," he said, "I was a soldier. Did I tell you about the war?"

"You said nasty things fell out of the sky," said Rosa, remembering.

"Did I?" he said. "You've got a good memory. Well now, when I was in Burma –"

"Where's Burma?"

"A long way away. The other side of the world. Where it's hot and steamy."

"Why were you in Burma,
Grandad?"

"Cos that's where they sent
me. You just eat your tea and
stop asking questions, or I'll
never get to the elephants."

Rosa took a little cake with
icing on and resolved not to
say another word.

"Now where was I?"

"In Burma," said Rosa, her mouth full of cake.

"In the jungle, yes. Sitting on an elephant. Hauling timber."

Rosa wasn't sure what hauling timber was, but she didn't dare ask.

"Hauling timber, that's what they used the elephants for. Pulling great tree trunks along. Wonderful beasts, elephants. Elephants never forget, did you know that, Rosa?"

Rosa nodded.

"Just like you," said Grandad. "And," he added,

"you can have another cake, if you like."

"Yes, please," said Rosa, and took one.

"Now, you just picture me," said Grandad, waving his hands about to make it seem more dramatic, "riding my elephant through the hot steamy jungle on my way back to the camp. And the sun's going down and there are these strange sounds of insects and birds and snakes and all sorts of animals."

"Weren't you frightened, Grandad?"

"Worst thing was the

leeches," he said. "Sucking your blood, nasty things."

Rosa made a face as if she'd just eaten something unpleasant.

"And then suddenly, on the path in front of us – what do you think? Two eyes blazing out of the darkness."

Rosa stopped eating her cake and looked at him. "What was it, Grandad? A monster? A dragon?"

"Tiger, tiger, burning bright, in the forests of the night," said Grandad. "You could hear it snarling. A man-eater, more than likely. Roaring and

growling. It was angry about something, all right."

Rosa's eyes grew bigger and bigger, and she quite forgot to eat the last piece of cake that she was holding in her hand. "What did you do, Grandad?"

"Only one thing to do," he said. "I sang it the loudest song I could think of. At the top of my voice. On wings of song I'll bear thee," he sang, "to those fair Asian lands, where the broad waves of the Ganges flows to its flowery strands. I pushed out my chest and I opened my mouth and I sang it so loud, it echoed through the great trees and up into the sky and all the jungle sounds went hush. Then my elephant started trumpeting and every living thing began making a terrible racket."

"What did the tiger do?" asked Rosa.

"Slunk off with its tail between its legs. What else? Don't think tigers like music much. Off it went into the darkness in full retreat. What do you think of that, Rosa?"

"You were very brave, Grandad."

"So I was," he said. "Cos they're powerful animals, tigers. Beautiful big cats.

That's how they move, like cats, so quietly and stealthily. Magnificent. But not in zoos. Tigers don't look right in zoos."

"I shan't go and see the tigers when I go to the zoo," said Rosa. "Just the monkeys. And the bears. And the elephants –" and she gave Grandad a worried, questioning look.

He laughed and patted her hand. "All right," he said. "If you insist, I'll come. After all, it might be the last chance I get to see an elephant anywhere."

"Oh, goody!" said Rosa,

clapping her hands. "I'm sure you'll have a lovely time."

"Grandad's coming with us to the zoo on Sunday," Rosa told her mother later that evening.

"Really?" Rosa's mother looked surprised. "I didn't think he liked zoos. He certainly never went with us when we were kids."

"He's seen elephants and tigers in the jungle," said Rosa.

"Is that what he told you?"

"Yes. And once he frightened a tiger away by singing."

Rosa's mum laughed. "You

can't believe everything your
old grandad tells you," she
said.

"But he said he did," Rosa
insisted.

"Well, maybe he did. You
never can tell with Grandad.
He tells so many stories. But
all I hope is he doesn't go

frightening any tigers in the zoo with his singing. You just make sure he doesn't get into any mischief, Rosa."

Rosa promised she'd look after him.

When Sunday came, it was dressed in a dull grey coat of clouds.

"Can we still go?" asked Rosa anxiously.

"Let's risk it," said her mum. "Better than being stuck in the house all day. Grandad's coming for lunch, so we'll leave as soon as we've finished. Better take an umbrella, though."

Lunch was roast lamb, which made Rosa feel a little sad, because she imagined the lambs she'd seen skipping about the fields and didn't much like the idea that she was now eating one of them. To make up for it, she decided she wouldn't eat any home-made apple pie, though it was her favourite pudding. "Eats like a bird," said Grandad, who had two helpings.

After lunch, they put on their hats and coats and Rosa and her mum took their umbrellas (but Grandad said he couldn't be bothered with

umbrellas) and they drove off to the zoo.

Whether it was the dull weather or because the animals had eaten a big lunch, Rosa didn't know, but none of the animals seemed to be doing very much. Many of them, like the wolves and the wombats, were inside their houses, asleep. The polar bears were stretched out on their rocks, looking bored. The elephants waved their trunks across the moat separating them from the watching crowds, as if sending out a distress signal. Even the monkeys did little more than scratch themselves or cling to the wire of the cage and watch the mums and dads and children who were watching them.

Rosa was disappointed and was beginning to pout. "Why aren't they doing things?" she complained.

"Maybe they don't feel like it," said Mum. "They're not obliged to, after all. And anyway, you're so impatient, you never stay watching them for long enough."

"It's boring when they're not doing anything."

"We could put you into the

lions' cage," said Grandad. "That might be exciting."

Rosa frowned.

"Or else," he went on, "we could go and find the parrots. I had a parrot once. Taught it to sing the 'Toreador's Song' from *Carmen*."

"Oh, yes?" said Rosa's mother. "When was that then?"

"Once upon a time," said Grandad vaguely.

"It must have been," she said. "Well, I'm going to have a cup of tea. My feet need a rest. You go off with Grandad and see the parrots, and then meet me in the café over there."

"Right," said Grandad. "I think the parrots are this way, little one."

And off they marched, hand in hand.

"What's the corridor song?" asked Rosa.

"The what?"

"What you said you taught your parrot," said Rosa.

"Oh, the 'Toreador's Song'," said Grandad. "A toreador is a bullfighter." And he raised his hat to the flamingos and sang, "Tor-e-ador, tor-e-ador –" The pink flamingos standing on one

leg in the pond lifted their long
curved necks to look at him,
and a cluster of pigeons in
front of them flew off, making
throat-rattling sounds.

"You mustn't frighten the
animals, Grandad," said Rosa.

"As if I would," he said.
"There's the parrot house. I

knew it was here somewhere."

They went inside and were nearly deafened by the noise of screeching and squawking and screaming and whistling from the blue and yellow macaws and the green and red parrots and the pink rosellas and the colourful lorikeets and the white cockatoos with the yellow crests on their heads.

"Why are they making such a noise?" asked Rosa.

"Maybe they're complaining because they're stuck in their cages on a Sunday afternoon when they'd rather be flying in the forest," said Grandad.

"Come on, let's ask this one."

They approached a large, beady-eyed green and red parrot, clinging to the cage wire.

"How do you do?" said Grandad to the parrot.

"How do you do?" said the parrot. "How's your father?"

"I haven't got a father," said Rosa.

"How's your father?" said the parrot again.

"Stupid parrot," said Rosa.

"You'll upset him," said Grandad. "Let's see if he'll sing us a song."

"Sing us a song," said the parrot.

"Any old iron," sang Grandad.

"Any old iron," echoed the parrot.

"Polly put the kettle on," sang Rosa.

"We'll all have tea," piped the parrot.

Rosa clapped her hands. "He can sing," she said. "Try teaching him that song about the bullfighter, Grandad."

"Tor-e-ador," sang Grandad.

The parrot cocked its head on one side and bit the wire of its cage angrily with its powerful, pointed beak.

"Come on, Polly. You can do it," said Grandad, and sang a bit louder, "Tor-e-ador –"

"Sam, Sam, dirty old man," squawked the parrot.

"Toreador," sang Grandad more loudly still.

"Sam, Sam, dirty old man,"

screeched the parrot again.

"Washed his face in a
frying-pan," sang Rosa,
jumping up and down
excitedly.

Grandfather tried again, but
the more he sang "Toreador",
the more the parrot responded
with "Sam, Sam, dirty old

man", until both of them
seemed to be getting quite
cross with each other. Soon
there was a crowd of children
and grown-ups round the cage,
applauding and urging them
on, and the other birds in the
parrot house started joining in
with a variety of squawks and

screeches and whistles and squeaks. The noise was like a great wave, and Rosa felt that she was almost drowning in it.

"Toreador," sang Grandfather at the top of his voice. He was going quite red in the face by now.

"Sam, Sam, dirty old man," screamed the parrot furiously.

Suddenly, just as Rosa was beginning to wonder how long they were going to keep this up, there was a loud blast on a whistle. Everybody turned round and saw the keeper walking towards them, looking stern.

"What's going on here?" he said.

"This blessed parrot," said Grandfather, "won't sing the 'Toreador's Song' from *Carmen*."

"Course he won't," said the keeper. "He hates opera. Used to belong to an operatic tenor.

Put him off it completely. Music hall songs. That's his speciality."

"In that case," said Grandfather with dignity, "I'm wasting my time." And he took Rosa's hand and led her out of the parrot house.

"How's your father?" they heard the parrot say as they went out the door.

"That was fun," said Rosa.

"That was thirsty work," said Grandad. "Let's go and find your mother and have a nice cup of tea."

So they did.

Grandfather
at the Seaside

"I don't know what I'm going to do with you," said Rosa's mother. "Don't you want a holiday?"

"Only if Grandad comes," said Rosa.

"Well, he can't," said her mother.

Rosa screwed up her eyes and clenched her hands. "I'm

not going," she said.

"Rosa!"

Rosa kept her eyes closed,
but she could feel the irritation
in her mother's voice.

"Sometimes," said Rosa's
mother, "I could shake you."

"Not going," said Rosa.

"Not without Grandad."

"He's old," said her mother.
"And he's not as well as he
was. I've told you. We can't
take him around with us
everywhere we go."

"He's my grandad," said
Rosa.

"I know he is," said her

mother. "But can't you do without him for two weeks? Don't you see enough of him at home? Rosa? I need a holiday, too, you know. Some time on my own. And with you. I don't want to have to look after him as well."

"He wouldn't be any trouble," said Rosa.

"Oh, wouldn't he!" said her mother. "I can just see him on the train, telling his stories to whoever'll listen. Embarrassing me. Singing away at the top of his voice in the guest-house. Complaining about the food. And the weather. Not like it used to be, that's what he'll say. I can just hear him. And I'm not having it."

"He needs a holiday," said Rosa. "He's peaky."

"Peaky, is he? How is he peaky?"

"That's what he told me," said Rosa. "I'm feeling a little peaky today. That's what he said."

Her mother sighed and looked at her daughter, sitting at the table with her half-eaten dinner in front of her and dirty tear-marks round her eyes. She didn't know what to say to her. She knew it was pointless

arguing with her. Stubborn,
she was. Once she'd got an
idea in her head. Just like you,
her father had said. She's got
your chin. And your wilful
ways. Once you'd got an idea
in your head, you wouldn't
listen to anybody. Still don't.
That's what her dad had said.

Rosa's grandad.

"Look, Rosa," she said. "Don't you think it would be nice if we spent some time together on holiday? We could do lovely things, paddling and building sandcastles and fishing for crabs and all sorts of things. Just me and you. Wouldn't you like that?"

Rosa unclenched her fists, opened her eyes and looked at her mother. Then her mouth turned down and her chin wobbled, and she suddenly burst into floods of tears. How she howled. Her mother picked her up and hugged her, but still

she howled and still the tears
flowed down until she could
hardly catch her breath.

"Come on, now, Rosa," said
her mother. "This isn't like
you. What are you crying like
that for? There's no need to cry
like that, is there? Big girl like
you. Look, I tell you what. If

you want Grandad to come
with us so much and if he's well
enough and if he wants to
come, we'll take him with us
for the first week. How about
that? Rosa? Come on, now.
Stop crying. Wipe your eyes.
And what about finishing your
dinner?"

So Rosa stopped crying and wiped her eyes with her handkerchief and gave her mother a kiss. "All right," she said. "Can I tell him?"

"You tell him," her mother said. "And remember, you'll have to look after him, because I won't."

When Rosa had finished her dinner, she went to the phone and dialled Grandad's number. She remembered it by heart. "Grandad," she said as soon as she heard his voice, "you're coming on holiday with us."

"Am I?" said Grandad's voice. "I didn't know that."

"Yes," said Rosa. "To the seaside. We're going paddling and fishing for crabs and building sandcastles. Don't you want to come?"

"Oh, I do like to be beside the seaside," sang Rosa's grandad's voice, "I do like to be beside the sea . . ."

"Just for one week, tell him," called Rosa's mother.

"Just for one week," said Rosa. "We're going for two. And my mum says it's a place called Swanage."

"I remember it well," said Grandad's voice.

"And tell him he's not to

sing on the train," called her
mother.

"Only you mustn't sing on
the train, Grandad," said
Rosa.

"As if I would," said
Grandad.

And he didn't. At least, not
until they were well out into

the countryside. And then he said he was only clearing his throat and exercising his larynx, but Rosa's mum said it sounded more like singing to her.

But when they got to the seaside, that was a different story. Every morning, the sun rose up into a clear blue sky, with just a few puffs of white cloud sailing across. And every morning when Grandad came down to breakfast, he sang "Good morning, good morning" to Rosa and her mother. And every morning Grandad looked out at the sparkling sunny day and said it was a small miracle, because the weather nowadays was usually nowhere near as nice as it had been when he was a boy.

And every morning, Rosa took her grandad down to the sea to let her mother finish her breakfast in peace. And

Grandad rolled his flannel trousers up and together they paddled in the waves and picked up pretty, patterned shells and stones that the waves had left behind along the shore. And when she asked him to sing the song about the seaside, he did, but not so loudly that anyone else could hear. "I do like to be beside the seaside," he sang, "I do like to be beside the sea."

At the end of the first week, Rosa and her mother were building a giant sandcastle by the deckchairs. Suddenly, Rosa's mother looked up.

"Where's Grandad?" she asked.

"He was reading. In the deckchair," Rosa said.

"Well, he's not there now, is he?" said her mother. "He's gone." And she looked anxiously up and down the sea-shore. "Where can he be?" she said.

There were other grandads and grandmas and mums and dads reading in their deckchairs or sunbathing with handkerchiefs over their faces. There were children running and chasing and fighting and throwing rubber rings and

kicking sand and footballs and
eating ice-creams and
ice-lollies. But no Grandad.

"Maybe he's swum out to
sea," said Rosa. "Maybe he's
swum to the other side of the
sea."

"I told you to keep an eye
on him," said her mother.

Suddenly, they heard a voice
rise up out of what seemed like
the middle of the sea. A strong
voice. A penetrating voice. A
singing voice. A Grandad
voice.

"That's Grandad," said
Rosa excitedly, clapping her
hands.

And there he was, his flannel trousers rolled up, sitting on a surfboard which was bobbing up and down on the waves a little way out to sea, singing away as if there was nobody else in the world. And as his voice soared over the water and circled the sea-shore, everybody stopped what they were doing to listen.

The children stopped playing and fighting and kicking footballs and eating their ice-creams and turned to stare out to sea. And the grown-ups in their deckchairs threw their hankies off their faces and sat bolt upright and shaded their eyes against the sun to try to spot where the voice was coming from. Even the seagulls stopped their squawking and fell silent.

"See the silver light shining on the waters. As fisherman gives maid a kiss of token," sang the voice as the wind carried it over the water. "When the moon rises over Marechiare . . ."

And when the voice had finished its song and the last notes had died away, a great cheer and shouts of Encore! Encore! swelled up along the sea-shore.

Rosa's mother raised her eyebrows and looked at her daughter. "I think," she said, "it's time he went home." Then she smiled a lovely warm smile that told Rosa that she wasn't really cross.

Silent Night

"I think we'd better leave Grandad behind this year," said Rosa's mother while they were having their breakfast.

Rosa looked doubtful.

"Remember what happened last year," said Rosa's mum.

"He enjoys coming," Rosa said. "He's pleased when I ask him."

"He enjoys it," said her mum. "But what about everybody else? I don't think your music teacher enjoyed it very much."

"He won't do it again," said Rosa. "I'm sure he won't."

"He'll say he won't," said her mum. "He'll promise he won't. But as soon as he hears the sound of his own voice, there'll be no holding him."

Rosa thought for a moment. She thought about the carol service the Christmas before. She thought of herself wearing her special blue dress, standing proudly in the front row of the

choir where everybody,
especially her mum and
grandad, could see her and
from where she could see
everybody, especially her mum
and grandad, dressed in their
smartest clothes and waiting to
hear her sing.

She remembered the carols
they'd sung and how the

audience were asked to sing
with the choir on certain songs
but not on others, which only
the school choir was supposed
to sing. And she remembered
how Grandad had joined in
with all the songs, even the
ones he wasn't supposed to
sing.

She'd watched her mum
trying to shush him, but
Grandad didn't seem to notice.
She could see him now, eyes
closed, singing away happily,
swept up by the music into a
world of his own, quite
unaware that everyone was
looking at him. He'd even

joined in with "Silent Night", a very quiet song which the choir had learned in two-part harmony.

"Silent night," sang the children sweetly.

"Holy night," her grandad's voice came chiming in from the audience.

"All is still," sang the choir, a little startled.

"All is bright," sang Grandad, in a voice that resonated through the hall.

So the choir sang more loudly, as if to blot out the voice that insisted on accompanying them from the audience. And Grandfather, who wasn't going to be outsung by a bunch of children, pushed out his chest, opened his mouth and, letting his voice come pouring out, sang more loudly still.

"Sleep in heavenly peace," they sang at the tops of their voices. Until by the end, the whole choir and Grandfather were bellowing so loudly and the noise was so great that some of the audience had put their fingers in their ears.

Rosa remembered how cross and red and flustered Mr Barnes, her music teacher, had been. "Well," he'd said, glaring at Grandad after the song was over and there was an embarrassed silence, "that was the noisiest 'Silent Night' I've ever heard."

And Rosa remembered looking at the floor and wishing she could disappear through it.

Rosa remembered all this and she sighed. "He'll be upset if he doesn't come," she said.

"I'll be upset if he does," said Mum. "And I don't know what Mr Barnes will say. Don't you remember how cross he was? If it hadn't been

Christmas and the season of
peace and goodwill, I dread to
think what he'd have done."

"But I want him to come,"

said Rosa. "It won't be the same without him."

"That's true," said Mum. "It won't. Why don't you ask your music teacher what he thinks? Maybe he can think of some way of keeping your grandfather quiet."

Rosa looked worried. "Won't you ask him, Mum?"

Her mother shook her head. "Nothing to do with me," she said. "Grandad's your problem. Come on or you'll be late for school."

"Did you talk to Mr Barnes?" asked Rosa's mum when she

met Rosa after school.

"Yes," said Rosa, as she
skipped along beside her
mother. "He said it's all right
for Grandad to come."

"On your head be it, Rosa.
But don't expect me to look
after him. I'll be sitting at the
opposite end of the hall,
pretending I don't know him."

"It's all right," said Rosa

and smiled mysteriously.

The first thing she did when she got home was to phone Grandad. She knew the number by heart.

"Grandad," she said when she heard his voice. "It's Rosa."

"Who?" asked Grandad.

"It's Rosa," said Rosa.

"Rosa? Which Rosa?"

"Grandad," said Rosa, "it's our carol concert tomorrow."

"God rest you merry gentlemen," sang Grandfather and chuckled.

"It's all right for you to come, Grandad."

"I wouldn't miss it for the world," said Grandad. "Ding, dong, merrily on high," he sang.

"Only you've got to come to the school at six o'clock," Rosa went on. "For a rehearsal."

"A rehearsal? Who says so?"

"My music teacher, Mr Barnes, said he's got something special for you to sing and would you come for a rehearsal with the choir at six o'clock."

"In that case," said Grandad, "I'll wear my bow-tie."

The school hall was brightly decorated and hung with paintings and mobiles. Mr Barnes played the piano with a flourish and the choir sang with enthusiasm. The audience of mothers and fathers and brothers and sisters and grandmothers and grandfathers joined in when they were asked to and didn't when they weren't. Rosa's mother looked around for Grandfather, but couldn't see him anywhere. What was more surprising was that she couldn't hear him either. Maybe he's fallen asleep, she thought. Or maybe he didn't come. Rosa will be disappointed.

Her eyes rested on Rosa, standing as tall as she could in the front row of the choir, looking bright and clean and singing her heart out. She felt tears coming into her eyes. Perhaps Rosa would have her

grandfather's voice. That
would be a mixed blessing. She
smiled to herself.

After everybody had
applauded "The Twelve Days
of Christmas", Mr Barnes
came on to the platform and
addressed the audience.
"Thank you very much," he

said. "We hope you've enjoyed our little concert. Now we have a surprise for you. We have invited a very special guest to sing with us on the last song, which will be 'Silent Night'. He's been waiting quietly and patiently in the wings and now it's time to welcome him on stage."

Mr Barnes went to a door at the back of the stage, opened it and called out: "You can come out now, Mr Shenstone." Then he turned to the audience and said: "Will you give a warm welcome to Rosa's grandfather, Mr Shenstone."

Everybody clapped and
cheered. Rosa went red and
looked at her feet.
Grandfather, wearing his
bow-tie, shuffled on to the
stage, acknowledging the
applauding audience with a
wave of his hand.

"Well, I'm blowed!" Rosa's
mother said to herself.
"They've never asked him to
sing."

But they had. And he did.
Taking his note from Mr
Barnes at the piano, he sang in
his softest, sweetest voice, his
closed eyes looking upwards,
the first verse of "Silent

Night". The choir joined him on the other verses and together they made the most beautiful sound.

When it was over, there was a hushed silence. Then the audience broke into wild applause, stamping their feet and filling the hall with their clapping and cheering. Grandfather bowed and took Rosa's hand and Rosa smiled and felt as bursting with happiness as she'd ever felt, and Rosa's friend Sam shouted, "Three cheers for Rosa's grandad," and all the boys and girls cheered and

laughed. Then it was all over.
It was time to go home.

Later that evening, when
Rosa was tucked up in bed, she
smiled at her mother and said:
"Mr Barnes said we sang like
angels."

"I've never heard angels
sing," said her mother, "but

I'm sure they don't sing half as well as you do."

"And Grandad was good, wasn't he?"

"Yes," said her mother, "I have to admit he was. The only thing is," she went on, "what are we going to do with him next year?"

"I can't wait till next year," said Rosa happily.

Her mother gave her a big kiss. "Sweet dreams," she said.

But the dream Rosa had was strange rather than sweet. She was floating through the blue sky with her angel wings on, playing a harp and singing.

And above her, sitting on a
cloud, was an old man with a
face that reminded her of
Grandfather. He was looking

rather cross and saying sternly:
"Sing louder! Sing louder!
Can't hear you!" And though
she was singing at the top of
her voice, no sound was
coming out and the
grandfather-man kept saying:
"Louder! Louder! You're not
singing loudly enough!" as she
floated helplessly and silently
through the blue of the sky.

Until she woke up.